SQUIRREL BOY Vs the Bogeyman

Dave Lowe

Illustrated by
Cate James

CONTENTS

Squirrel Boy vs the Bogeyman

ISBN: 978-1-907-912-72-6

Published in the UK by Phoenix Yard Books Ltd
This edition published 2015

Phoenix Yard Books
Phoenix Yard
65 King's Cross Road
London
WC1X 9LW

Text copyright © Dave Lowe, 2015
Illustrations copyright © Cate James, 2015

Design by Katie Bennett @ Kreative Cupboard

1 3 5 7 9 10 8 6 4 2

Printed in the UK

A CIP catalogue record for this book is available from the British Library

www.phoenixyardbooks.com

To Stacey. I'm nuts about you.

Walter Kettle was a normal kid, just like you, until he went out into the garden one day and the really, really bad thing happened.

No one was to blame, not really. But if you wanted to blame anything, I suppose you could blame Brussels sprouts. His mum was boiling some for dinner, and the smell of boiling Brussels sprouts was one of Walter's least favourite things in the world.

So he went out into the garden to get some fresh air. The garden was long, narrow and sloping, with fences either side, a big, leafy tree down the bottom and nothing at all to play with.

His only outside toy was a ball, and that was stuck right up the top of the tree. He didn't have any brothers or sisters or pets, or even a dad, to play with, and he was much too shy to ask any of the neighbours' kids to play. So he just sat

CHAPTER TWO

Nothing happened.

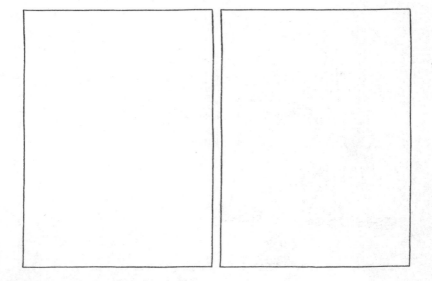

CHAPTER THREE

I'm sorry about Chapter Two but, really, for twenty-seven and a half minutes, nothing of any interest happened.

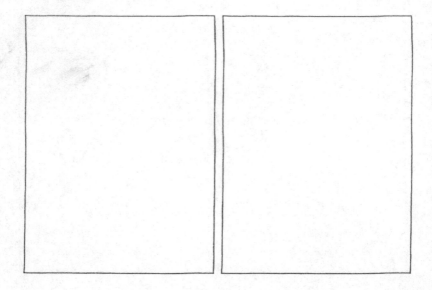

He just sat there, under the tree, looking at the grass, hoping for a worm or a bug to appear, so he would have something to watch.

But no creatures came out. Not one. Not even an ant. Not even a baby ant.

So, apologies for Chapter Two, but keep reading, because Chapter Four is going to be absolutely brilliant. Lots of exciting things happen: things that completely change Walter Kettle's life.

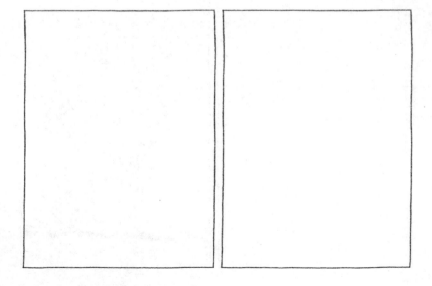

CHAPTER FOUR

It started when a nut fell on Walter's head.

"Ouch!" he said, wincing. Then he rubbed his head and looked up in surprise.

You'd be surprised, too, if you were sitting under a tree and a nut smacked you on the head. But Walter was doubly surprised because the tree he was sitting under wasn't even a nut tree. It was just a regular tree, with lots of leaves and branches, but definitely no fruit or nuts.

When he looked up, he saw leaves rustling, but he couldn't make out what was making them rustle. It wasn't windy. He frowned, then shrugged and examined the nut that had fallen.

He wasn't much of a nut expert – not many ten year olds are – but it looked to him like a hazelnut and, with nothing better to do, he decided to crack open the shell.

Hazelnuts, however, are very tough nuts to crack. He couldn't do it with his hands, so he stood up and stamped on it. This didn't work either, so he picked up a branch from the ground and started whacking the nut with it. This is when he heard another rustle. He looked up again. Whatever was in the tree – a bird? – had come closer.

He shrugged again and went back to hitting the nut with the branch.

And then, out of nowhere, came a squirrel. The squirrel didn't look at all pleased.

If you saw someone hitting something of yours with a stick, you'd be pretty angry, too.

Walter Kettle didn't know what hit him

(apart from the nut, of course).

The squirrel leapt from the lower branches of the tree and landed on Walter's head.

Walter yelped and tossed his head about wildly to shake the squirrel off. But the squirrel clung on, before scampering down Walter's back and biting him on the bottom.

"Ow! Ow! Ouch!" said Walter, because squirrels have needle-sharp claws... and teeth.

Then he watched in shock as the angry squirrel darted between his legs, rescued the nut and raced back up the tree.

Poor Walter.

He has only said four words in this story so far, and all of them have been

"Ow!" or "Ouch!"

But I'm afraid that things were about to get worse for Walter Kettle.

CHAPTER FIVE

Walter's mum is a vegetarian. She loves animals, works for a charity called Friends of the Animals, and even writes their blog, called *All About Animals*.

Being vegetarian is actually a very kind thing, to animals, and to the environment. And vegetarian food can be really delicious. But not the vegetarian food that Walter's mum makes.

Today, like every Wednesday, they had nut roast, Brussels sprouts and broccoli.

We've already discussed sprouts, and the less said about them the better.

Nut roast is not too bad: it's like meatloaf except that it's made with nuts and isn't quite as tasty.

As for broccoli... well, it looks like a cartoon fart. And you should never, ever eat something that looks like a cartoon fart. But Walter, as usual, ate most of what was on his plate. He was good like that.

As they were clearing the table afterwards, his mum asked how his day had been. Walter finally said something in this story that wasn't "ow!" or "ouch!"

"Not bad," he said, deciding that it was best not to tell her about the squirrel attack. She probably wouldn't believe him, anyway.

After dinner, Walter and his mum were watching the local news on TV. The main story was about a small explosion in the nuclear power plant, which wasn't far from the Kettle house.

Walter's mum tutted and shook her head, and he knew exactly what she'd say: "The sooner we all use wind power," she said, on cue, "the better."

Walter nodded. He guessed that, seeing how many lentils and beans he and his mum ate every week, they could probably start up a wind farm themselves.

The reporter on TV was standing outside the power plant and saying that nobody had been hurt in the explosion. And that was true. But what they didn't know was that there was one intrepid animal who had been affected.

A squirrel.

And it was a squirrel that Walter Kettle had already met.

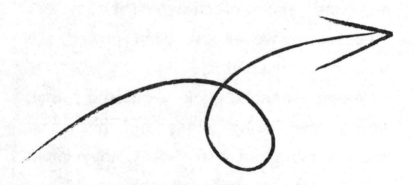

CHAPTER SIX

The TV news moved onto the next story, about a local man who had broken the world record for eating jelly babies: 217 in a minute.

"Revolting!" Walter's mum was saying. "It makes me feel queasy just thinking about it."

But Walter was feeling queasy himself, and it wasn't the jelly baby world record that was making him feel that way. He went to his room and sat on his bed.

And that's when something very strange indeed started to happen to him.

First, he started to twitch.

It was just his nose to begin with; the tiniest tickle. He rubbed it with the back of a finger, but the sensation didn't stop. In fact, very soon his entire face felt prickly and tickly. Then his shoulders. It wasn't long before his whole body felt like that, and he was writhing and wriggling... and very scared indeed.

And suddenly his lower back was burning, as if he was standing too close to a fire.

He leapt from the bed and stared wild-eyed into the full-length mirror, expecting to see some kind of rash.

But what he actually saw took his

breath away.

He had a tail.

And not just any tail: a huge, bushy tail. It started from just above his bottom, and stood up higher than his head, the tip of it curving away from him, like a question mark.

Walter Kettle wasn't very talkative at the best of times. But now he stood staring at himself in the mirror, so utterly shocked that he was unable to even make a sound.

Then he noticed something else unusual.

As I'm sure you can imagine, when a gigantic, bushy tail has suddenly sprouted out of you, 'something else' would have to be pretty unusual indeed in order for you to notice it.

Something incredibly strange had happened to his face. His cheeks, in fact:

they were puffy and swollen, like he'd stuffed each one with a ping-pong ball.

And it was when he touched his cheeks that he noticed one more alarming thing: his fingernails had suddenly grown... curved and sharp and pointy. In fact, they looked less like fingernails and more like claws.

Walter took a deep breath, studied his reflection some more, and sat down on his bed in a state of complete shock.

CHAPTER SEVEN

On that same day, a man on the other side of town was picking his nose.

Now, this might not seem to you like a very useful piece of information. Also, it's pretty disgusting. But, believe me, of all the noses in all the world that were being picked at that very moment, this particular nose was by far the most important.

The owner of the nose (and finger) was a man called Jeremy Winkleman-Grubb. He was thirty-three years old and still lived with his mum.

Jeremy Winkleman-Grubb, like quite a lot of grown-ups, was mostly interested in money. But he was also very lazy and, instead of actually working hard to get that money, he spent most of the day dreaming up get-rich-quick schemes, eating junk food, watching the telly and, of course, picking his nose.

He didn't just watch the telly either: he shouted abuse at it, too.

At exactly the same time that Walter Kettle was being attacked by the squirrel, Jeremy Winkleman-Grubb was watching a quiz show.

"You, Madam, have a face like a chimpanzee's bottom!" he yelled at one contestant. And when the next contestant got an answer wrong, he shouted: "You, Sir, are stupider than a whelk."

And then, feeling very pleased with himself, he inserted his right index finger (his favourite picking finger) into his right nostril, and had an extremely thorough rummage around.

"Stop picking yer nose!" barked his mum, who was sprawled in an armchair opposite him.

"I was just scratching!" he snarled.

"Your finger was so far up there," she snapped, "that if you were scratching anything, it was probably yer brain. If you've got one, that is."

His mother was an entirely different shape to him: he was tall and skinny, whereas she was so round that she was practically spherical. Their personalities, however, were very similar indeed.

He took his finger out of his nose and examined the contents, as if he'd been digging for treasure and was checking what he'd unearthed.

But it was something he'd put in his nose that was the problem.

You see, on his fingernail, just before he'd poked it into his nostril, there was the tiniest bug: more of a speck, actually; so incredibly small that you would have needed a microscope to see it.

And this particular bug had, until recently, been living in the armpit of a squirrel. A squirrel we have already met.

Like the squirrel, the bug was now radioactive.

The explosion had blown the bug away from the squirrel and it had floated in the breeze, across the town, through a window and into the Winkleman-Grubb household.

Maybe you're wondering: what happens when a tiny radioactive bug ends up being rammed into your nostril?

Well, the bug dies instantly. (And the next time you complain about your life, just be thankful that you're not a bug that has spent most of its short life in a squirrel's armpit and ended it squashed up some-one's nose.)

But more importantly for our story, something very strange indeed was about to happen to Jeremy Winkleman-Grubb.

CHAPTER EIGHT

Which Is Not Really A Chapter But More Of A Warning.

I should warn you, the next chapter is pretty disgusting. If you're eating (and especially if you're eating something runny, like custard), you might want to finish it before turning the page.

CHAPTER NINE

Two minutes and twelve seconds after picking his nose, Jeremy Winkleman-Grubb felt a strange tingling sensation.

It started in his nostril and then the tingling – like pins and needles – swept over his face, down his spine and, before long, had spread down to his toes. By now, he was really freaking out.

"Mummy!" he shrieked.

"Shush!" she snapped. "I'm trying to watch the television!"

"I feel terrible," he moaned.

She sighed, and finally tore her gaze away from the screen to look at him.

She gasped.

Something was wrong with him. Very wrong indeed.

His skin had turned a sickly green colour. And, more than that: his face and hands were covered in... what? At first, she thought it looked like sweat, but it was thicker than that.

"What's happening to me?!" he yelped, his voice wobbling.

"You're a funny colour," she informed him. "And you're all covered in… goo."

He inspected one of his hands. She was right. It was covered with a sticky film, and it was the colour of... well, there was

no other way of saying it: snot. His entire body was the same; the goo was seeping through his clothes.

He touched his forehead, felt globules of icky gloop and then started gibbering and whimpering.

And what happened next only made him much, much worse.

His left leg stretched out. But not just a bit. Not like you or I would stretch our legs out. No. His leg stretched out and out and out, like it was made of elastic. It went as far as the television, swerved around it and came back to him in a loop.

Then, incredibly, his right hand whooshed out even further, snaking out into the hall.

He stared open-mouthed at his

elastic limbs.

His mum, meanwhile, was not so much giggling as gurgling with laughter. It was the funniest thing she'd seen since the old man over the road had stood in a huge, squelchy dog poo.

"What's going on?" Jeremy Winkle-man-Grubb managed to say, through his own whimpers and his mum's whoops of laughter.

"I don't know how or why," she said, hooting with delight, "but it seems very much like you've turned into..."

"Into a what?" he yelled, impatiently.

"A human bogey!" she announced, clapping her hands with glee.

CHAPTER TEN

You might be wondering what has been happening to Walter Kettle since we last saw him, sitting on his bed in a state of shock and looking like some kind of squirrel person. Well, fifty-three minutes later, he's still there, in exactly the same position.

After almost an hour of utter disbelief, Walter found that some questions had eventually elbowed their way into his mind. Questions like:

1. What am I going to do?

2. What will my mum do when she sees me like this? and

3. Will the kids at school make fun of me?

(The answers were 1. No idea. 2. Faint. 3. Oh, yes.)

It was then that he started to cry.

As tears rolled down his cheeks, though, something surprising and quite wonderful happened: his tail curled over his shoulder and dried his face.

It tickled, and he couldn't stop a chuckle escaping.

And then he started wondering what else his tail could do.

He stood up and swished it left and right, up and down, around and around in circles. It felt incredibly strong and he wondered just how strong it was: he piled five schoolbooks on it and found he could lift them easily, then flipped them like pancakes and caught them. It was a truly remarkable tail: not only powerful, but flexible and dextrous, too. He grinned as he tossed the books higher and higher. And then they hit the ceiling and tumbled crashing to the floor.

"Is everything okay up there, Walter?" called his mum from downstairs.

"Yes," he answered quickly.

But everything was definitely

not okay. Not okay at all. He was half-squirrel! And now he could hear his mum coming upstairs.

It was then that he felt the same tingly, prickly sensation sweep over his body, and when he jumped up and looked in the mirror, he saw that his body was changing rapidly back to normal: the tail shrank until it had completely disappeared; and his fingernails and cheeks were no longer at all squirrel-ish.

His mum came in, saw the books scattered on the floor and frowned.

"I dropped them," he said.

"You are clumsy, Walter," she said with a smile and, after she'd gone, he sighed with relief, sagged back onto his bed and tried to understand what was going on.

People sometimes think that shy kids aren't so intelligent. But this is a big mistake: the quiet ones are often the cleverest. In no time at all, Walter worked out what had happened to him.

He had read *Spiderman* comics and watched the films, so he knew that Spiderman was really a normal kid called Peter Parker, who'd been bitten by a radioactive spider.

Walter guessed that the same thing must have happened to him, except it was a squirrel that had bitten him.

What he didn't understand, though, was why the squirrel transformation had come and gone like that. And also, why had it happened more than an hour after the squirrel attack itself?

But Walter was smart, and it didn't take him very long to work it out.

CHAPTER ELEVEN

All the next week, at school and at home – he stayed out of the garden – Walter didn't feel in the least bit squirrel-ish. Not a twitch. Nothing.

But he thought about what had happened, of course. He thought about it almost all of the time. It's incredibly hard to concentrate on Maths or Music – or anything, really – when you've recently turned into a squirrel.

Exactly one week after the squirrel

incident, Walter and his mum were eating dinner. It was Wednesday, which meant it was nut roast and broccoli and sprouts again.

"You've been really quiet, recently," his mum said. "Even quieter than usual, I mean."

Walter swallowed a piece of nut roast, and shrugged.

"Anything you'd like to talk about?" she asked.

He shook his head. He would have liked to talk to someone about the whole squirrel thing, but it was a very difficult subject to bring up. Plus, his mum worried about him at the best of times.

After dinner, he thanked his mum, as usual, helped clear the table and

went to his room.

And then he turned into a squirrel.

It happened exactly the same way as before: the twitching; the prickly, burning sensation; the cheeks; the fingernails; the huge tail sprouting.

This time, though, it wasn't quite as much of a shock, so he spent slightly less time freaking out, and more time investigating the changes that had happened. He swished his tail around and then took his socks off to check out his feet. His toenails, as he'd suspected, had turned claw-like, too.

And he also noticed something else this time: his sense of smell had become a lot more powerful. For example, although his bedroom window was closed, he could smell delicious roast chicken and gravy wafting from the house next door, where old Mrs Onions lived. Then he sniffed again. What was that? The spices tickled his nostrils. It was a curry from the Nareds' house, two doors down. A lamb curry, if he wasn't mistaken, with tomato and garlic and chilli.

Impressed with his new-found ability, he wondered if he could smell even further.

He sniffed deeply.

Oh dear.

Dog poo.

It was Bruce, the Smiths' terrier, from three houses away.

Walter decided that a squirrely sense of smell might not be the best gift, after all.

As he tried to shake the smell of dog poo from his mind, he pondered why it was that he only turned into a squirrel on Wednesday evenings, and wondered if he was going to spend the rest of his life being half-squirrel at this time every week.

He really, really hoped not.

CHAPTER TWELVE

Walter's mum believed in healthy food for every meal, and breakfast was no exception. The other kids in Walter's class had Choco-Flakes or Honey Bombs or Sugar-Crunch Crispies: cereals that were delicious but incredibly bad for you.

In the Kettle house, however, the breakfast cereals all came in beige packets with names like Healthy Bran or Nice 'n' Fibre, and always tasted of soggy cardboard.

But this morning, in the kitchen in his pyjamas, Walter saw a new box in the cupboard; a cereal he hadn't seen before: 'Nut-ricious'. It was still in a rather dull packet, but it looked a little more promising.

He poured himself a bowlful and added the milk; skimmed milk, of course. The new cereal was pretty bland, but the tiny flecks of nut on top of the bran flakes did at least make it a bit tastier. Soggy cardboard with added nuts, he decided, tasted a teeny bit better than soggy cardboard on its own.

It was after he'd finished his breakfast and was in the bathroom brushing his teeth, that he felt a by-now familiar twitch.

This can't be happening, he thought, panicking. Not on a Thursday morning.

Not just before school.

But it was happening.

He immediately locked the bathroom door and watched himself transform in the mirror.

There was the huge tail popping out.

There were the claw-like fingernails growing.

There were the puffed out cheeks appearing.

He stared at his reflection, hoping he would change back more quickly this time.

He didn't.

To make matters even worse, his mum was impatiently yelling his name from the bottom of the stairs.

"Walter! Hurry up and get dressed! You'll be late for school!"

"I'm sick, Mum!" Walter called out, and then heard her footsteps as she rushed up the stairs.

"What's wrong?" she asked, from outside the bathroom door.

A lot was wrong, he thought, seeing his tail swish behind him in the mirror. But instead he said: "I've got a headache, Mum."

"Can I come in?"

"You go to work, Mum. I'll be okay here."

"Let me in," she said, kindly but firmly.

Walter had an idea.

"Can you get me an aspirin, please?" he asked.

The aspirin was in the kitchen cupboard and, as soon as he heard her bounding downstairs, he quickly unlocked the bathroom door, tiptoed to his room, snatched the curtains shut and jumped into bed.

He tucked his tail under the pillow, pulled the bedsheets above his nose and waited nervously for his mum to come back with the aspirin and a glass of water, which she placed on the bedside table.

She felt his forehead.

"Ooh, you're on fire," she said, and it was true that Walter's temperature went up after the transformation: a squirrel's body temperature is much higher than ours.

"Poor you." She sighed. "I'll have to take the day off work."

"It's okay," he croaked. "I just need some rest. Go to work, Mum. I'll be fine."

She thought about it for a while.

"Okay," she said. "If you're sure. But I'll pop next door and ask Mrs Onions to keep an eye out for you."

She kissed him on the forehead, and left.

Lying in bed, Walter sighed with relief. Being a pretty smart kid, he had already worked out what made him transform into a squirrel:

Nuts.

Anything nutty.

The nut roast, and now the breakfast cereal.

The important thing was that he'd escaped being found out by his mum, and now that he knew what made him change into a squirrel, he could stop it from happening again. All he had to do was avoid nuts. No big deal. Deborah Palmer in his class was allergic to nuts and milk and seafood, and she seemed to manage just fine.

And then Walter had a thought: If this is the last time I ever become a squirrel, he decided, I may as well see what I can do.

So he leapt out of bed and, still in his pyjamas, rushed into the garden.

CHAPTER THIRTEEN

Each time he picked his nose, Jeremy Winkleman-Grubb's body would become all gooey and stretchy for eleven-and-a-half minutes, before returning to normal.

But then he'd absent-mindedly shove a finger back up his nose, and the whole process would begin again.

It took the Winkleman-Grubbs several days to work out quite what was going on, and Jeremy Winkleman-Grubb was getting more and more upset, but far too

nounced, one

ie air.

you turn all

g. "It's picking yer

nose. se," she explained,

"and then you ci e. I always said it was

a filthy habit," she added, with a burp.

He stared at his mother, his brow creased in concentration.

Now, you or me, if we were unfortunate enough to turn into a kind of mutant bogey every time we picked our nose, would certainly give up the habit. But Jeremy Winkleman-Grubb was not like you or me.

His eyes widened. And then, very

deliberately, he picked his nose.

Sure enough, two minutes later, he was turning the by-now-familiar snot colour, slimy goo oozing out of his pores, and his limbs suddenly all stretchy.

"You're right, woman!" he exclaimed, adding: "For once."

By now it had happened so often that he'd trained his limbs to go exactly where he wanted them. This time, his right hand snaked out into the kitchen, opened the fridge and came back clutching a chocolate bar, while his left hand shot out to pinch his mother's arm.

"Ow!" she yelped, her face turning red with anger. "Next time you do that, I'll…"

But he wasn't listening. A dreamy expression had taken over his horrible, gooey face.

"I've got a plan," he said. "A plan to make us incredibly rich. Just think how easy it would be for these stretchy arms of mine to steal things: from people's bags; from cash registers; even from banks. Best of all, I wouldn't even need a disguise, because no one would ever recognise me. And my body will be so flexible that I won't be caught."

He grinned, hideously.

"I'll show them," he said.

"Show who?"

"All those people at school, who doubted me: the teachers who didn't give me As; the kids who didn't like me, who said I was a bully; the girls who called me 'Stinkleman-Grubb' – I'll show them. I'd love to see the looks on their idiotic fac-es, if they knew I'd become a criminal mastermind."

His mother cackled approvingly.

"All that you need," she said, "is a name."

He sighed.

"You've already given me five of them, woman," he moaned. "Jeremy Horatio Bartholomew Winkleman-Grubb. I'm full up with names."

"What I mean is," she said, rolling her eyes, "if you're going to be some kind of supervil-lain, you need a special name. What about 'The Human Bogey'?"

"I don't want to be 'The Human Bogey'," he snapped.

"How about 'SuperSnot', then?" she suggested.

"Absolutely not."

"'Mucus Man'?"

He reached out his stretchy left arm and pinched her hard on the leg.

"Ow!" she said, followed by several less polite words.

"I've got it!" he announced, slime oozing disgustingly from every pore. "You can call me 'the Bogeyman'!"

CHAPTER FOURTEEN

Walter didn't worry about his neighbours seeing him, because there were fences on either side of the garden. He didn't even bother covering up his tail, which was poking out of the back of his pyjamas.

He looked up at the ball that was stuck in the top branches of the tree, and wondered if he could get it. There was only one way to find out.

He stepped over to the tree, gripped the trunk and took a deep breath. Normally, he was terrified of heights and he wasn't at all good at climbing.

This made what happened next all the more incredible.

He raced up the tree, dodging branches, his arms and legs propelling him powerfully upwards until, only seconds later, he was right at the top. He plucked the ball from where it had been wedged for months, threw it to the ground, and then he scampered back down, even faster than he'd climbed.

Back on the grass, he was out of breath and utterly exhilarated.

Then his heart almost stopped.

"Walter?"

He looked around, panicking. He couldn't see anyone. He recognised the voice, though: an old lady's voice. Mrs Onions.

She must have been in the garden next door, he thought, but surely she couldn't see him. He double-checked that there were no gaps in the fence.

And then he realised just how stupid he'd been. The fences stopped people seeing into the garden, yes. But when he was climbing the tree, anyone could have seen him. And someone did. Mrs Onions.

"Are you there, Walter?" she asked. "Is that you?"

"Yes," he said, weakly.

"Your mum said you were sick."

"I am," he mumbled.

"You didn't look sick," she said, "when you were bolting up that tree just now."

He didn't speak. "I was pruning my geraniums," she continued, "when I heard the noise. I looked up and thought it must have been a squirrel, but it was much, much too big, and then I saw it was you, going incredibly quickly."

"Please don't tell my mum."

"Come over to my house," she said, not unkindly, "and explain yourself."

"Okay," he said, thinking that by the time he'd got dressed he might be back to normal again, and then he'd probably be able to make up a good excuse. "I'll just get changed," he said.

"Not likely," she said, with a laugh. "Come round here this instant. You're up to something, young man, and I'd very much like to know what. There's never anything good on telly during the day," she added, "so I have to take my entertainment where I can get it."

CHAPTER FIFTEEN

Mrs Onions was not your average old lady.

She often smoked a pipe, she'd had lots of amazing jobs, and she'd visited a lot of different countries. She'd been to Austria and Antigua, to Azerbaijan and Angola, and that was just the As.

But she certainly looked like a typical old lady, that was true: she had short grey hair, wore glasses and had a slow, hobbly way of walking.

She'd only just got to the front door when Walter arrived in his pyjamas and a dressing gown he'd quickly pulled on, which concealed his tail.

He hoped that, like a lot of older people, her eyesight wasn't great and so she wouldn't notice just how much he looked like a squirrel.

But when she opened the door, her eyes nearly popped out of her head.

"Jiminy Christmas!" she exclaimed. "Look at your cheeks, young man! Have you got the mumps?"

He sighed with relief.

That's it, he thought. That would explain the puffy cheeks, alright.

He nodded eagerly, happy that his secret would still be safe.

And that's when his bushy tail sprang out of its hiding place, and towered suddenly above his head.

There was a very uncomfortable silence. At first, Walter thought she was going to faint, at the very least, or have a heart attack, at worst.

She stared at his face, shook her head, looked up at the tip of the tail, shook her head again, and then squinted at his face again.

"I think I need a cup of tea," she said, eventually.

CHAPTER SIXTEEN

Walter had never been in Mrs Onions' front room before. The walls were decorated with dozens of framed photographs – so many that you could hardly see the wallpaper – and they were all of Mrs Onions herself. She'd obviously lived an incredible life. Above the fireplace, for example, was a picture of her in front of a pyramid, and then a photo of her in a karate uniform with a black belt. Next was Mrs Onions in

a white tennis dress, holding a racquet in one hand and a trophy in the other. Then came a photo of her in the cockpit of a small aeroplane. And next to that was a picture of her many years ago, wearing a glamorous dress and standing next to a man who Walter vaguely recognised. In the picture, the young Mrs Onions and the man were both grinning.

"Who's that next to you?" Walter asked, pointing.

She put down her cup of tea, looked up at the photo, and said:

"That is Mr Neil Armstrong, the first man to walk on the moon."

"Wow!" he said, and was about to ask her lots of questions about him, when she interrupted:

"Could we possibly discuss my photographs another time, Walter? Because we seem to have a far more pressing matter at hand; that being – and there's really no other way to say this – you seem to be half-squirrel."

He nodded, and told her everything.

"Wow," she said.

"Please don't tell anyone," he pleaded.

"Not even your mum?" she said.

"Especially not my mum. She worries too much as it is. Finding out that her son turns into a squirrel might kill her."

Mrs Onions thought about it for a while.

"Okay," she said, eventually. "I'll keep it to myself."

"Promise?"

"I have kept the secrets of world leaders, young man," she said. "I can undoubtedly keep–"

She stopped suddenly because, in front of her eyes, Walter's tail started shrinking to nothing, and the rest of his body went back to normal, too: his face, hands and feet.

"Incredible," she said, and added: "I suppose that all you need to do now is avoid nuts."

He nodded.

And that would have been the end of this story... if it hadn't been for Jeremy Winkleman-Grubb.

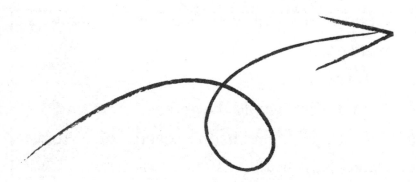

CHAPTER EIGHTEEN

Meanwhile, Walter's life went on as normal. Or, at least, as normal as possible when you know that you are only one nut away from turning into a squirrel. At school, he was a little more distracted, but was basically the same quiet, shy kid he'd been before the whole squirrel thing.

Then, one Wednesday afternoon, as he was doing science homework in his bedroom, there was a knock at the front door, and everything changed.

His mum answered the door, and said, in a big happy voice, "Mrs Onions! Very nice to see you! Please come in!"

Walter gasped. Mrs Onions hardly ever came round to visit, and he was suddenly very worried that she'd come to tell his mum the secret. His heart was beating incredibly fast as he scampered downstairs and, in the hall, he stared at the old lady, stunned.

"Can I help you with something, Mrs Onions?" said Walter's mum, smiling.

"Actually," said the old lady, "it was Walter that I came to see. I was hoping he could help me with some jobs in exchange for a bit of pocket money. If that's okay with you, and him, of course."

Walter was filled with relief, and his

mum was nodding encouragingly.

"So, Walter," Mrs Onions said. "What do you think?"

"Sure," he said. His mum beamed with pride that he was doing something nice for an elderly neighbour.

"He can eat at mine, if that suits," Mrs Onions said, and Walter nodded eagerly. It was broccoli and Brussels sprouts night at home.

"Be good," said his mum, and Walter went back with his next-door neighbour to her house.

"Take a seat," Mrs Onions said, gesturing to a comfy armchair in her front room. "I'll get you a lemonade." Walter sat nervously until she came back with the drink. "It's homemade," she said.

He took a sip. It was delicious.

Mrs Onions sat down opposite him, and smiled.

"I wasn't exactly telling the truth when I said I had some jobs for you, Walter. It's actually one big job. And it's not just for me. It's for everyone. The whole town. The world, in fact."

"Oh?"

"You've heard, no doubt, about the criminal who calls himself 'the Bogeyman.'" Walter nodded. It was the only thing that everyone at school was talking about. "Nothing is safe," Mrs Onions continued. "The whole town is in a panic, and the police seem to be powerless. What we need," she said, "is some kind of superhero."

He looked blankly at her.

"I'm talking about you, Walter."

"Me?" he said, astonished. "But I just grow a tail, and stuff. I'm not–"

"That tail of yours," she said, "is incredibly strong; a very powerful weapon. You can climb extremely fast. Your sense of smell is amazing. And, like a squirrel, I bet you'll be able to leap for metres, too."

"But I'm only a boy."

"Not only a boy. You're 'Squirrel Boy'!" she announced. "Like Batman or Spiderman, but younger, and more squirrely."

"They're comic book characters," he said. "I'm a real kid."

"I'm glad to hear it," she said, and then she pointed to a photo on the wall, the one he'd asked her about last time. "Neil

Armstrong wasn't a character from a comic. He was just a kid once upon a time. And he ended up going to the moon. Kids," she added, "even ones without superpowers, have the ability to change the world."

Walter sighed.

"Your country needs you," she said, slowly, looking into his eyes.

"Okay," he said, eventually. "I'll try."

"Good lad. First things first," she said. "We need a costume for you. A cape, for example, or a pair of tights with underpants on the outside."

He shook his head, blushing.

"A cape would look really silly," he said. "And there is absolutely no way I'm wearing tights. And pants are definitely not meant to be worn on the outside. That's why they're called *under-pants*."

"Okay," she said. "You could be right

about those things. But you definitely need a mask. Otherwise, somebody might recognise you."

She stood up, went to the fridge, refilled his glass with lemonade and brought him a large slice of homemade meat pie. He took a bite. It was completely delicious, bursting with chunks of steak and veg. She left him with the pie and went to her sewing room to make the mask. Half an hour later, the meat pie was finished, and so was the mask.

She handed it to him with a flourish.

"Yellow?" he said, screwing up his face.

"What's wrong with yellow?"

"Well, it's not the most exciting colour, is it?"

"You're Squirrel Boy," she said.

"And Squirrels are brown, which is not the most exciting colour in the world. We need a colour that makes you stand out."

"Then again," she pondered, "Bats are black, and Batman wears black."

"What about Spiderman, though?" he said. "Most spiders are black, or brown, but his costume is red and blue, and it looks really cool."

"Good point," she said. "The truth is, I had some yellow material left over from a banana costume I made. So, yellow it is."

He tried it on and looked at himself in the mirror. It looked pretty silly, but at least it was a good fit.

"So, that's the costume finished," she said, proudly.

"I've been wondering," said Walter, "how

we're going to find the Bogeyman."

Mrs Onions grinned.

"Come with me," she said, lit her pipe, and hobbled over to the dining table.

CHAPTER NINETEEN

On the dining table, Mrs Onions had spread out newspaper cuttings, and unfolded a map of the town.

"This," she said, puffing on her pipe and putting a sticker on the map, "is where he went on Sunday." She shook her head, sadly. "Arj at the corner shop is a lovely man; always has a smile and a special offer on baked beans. Here's the bakery, where he went on Tuesday. And the toy shop yesterday. Have you been there?"

Walter nodded. His mum occasionally took him there on a Saturday when he'd saved up enough pocket money. The lady who ran the shop was very nice, and he hated to think of her being terrified (and covered in goo) by the Bogeyman.

"Today," Mrs Onions continued, placing a final sticker onto the map, "they're reporting that he went to Dickson's, the jeweller's, and snatched money and handfuls of gold necklaces. Now, tell me what pattern you notice."

Walter studied the map.

"They're all in the same area," he said.

"That's right," she said. "What else?"

He shrugged, so she answered her own question.

"He's getting more ambitious each time.

The bakery is bigger than the corner shop, the toy shop is bigger than the bakery, and the jeweller's, of course, has the most valuable goods of all. Also, there is something very interesting about the names of the places he robs. Arj's. The Bakery. Celia's Toy Emporium. Dickson's."

"ABCD!" Walter exclaimed. "He's going through the alphabet!"

"Got it in one," she said, with a grin. "It seems that the Bogeyman is trying to show off; to show everyone how smart he is. So, where do you think he'll go tomorrow?"

Walter thought about it for a while.

"EasyBuy!" he said. "The supermarket! It's bigger, and begins with an E."

"Exactly. And it has many, many cash registers, with lots and lots of money."

"But, wait. I'm at school tomorrow," said Walter.

"Aah. But that's the other thing I noticed from reading the newspapers. He always strikes in the afternoon; at four or five. And I have a theory about that too."

Walter wasn't at all surprised to hear that.

"Actually," she said, "I have three theories: either he's very lazy and can't get out of bed; or he's waiting for the cash registers to fill up with money; or he's a real show-off, and wants to commit his crimes in front of as many people as possible; or maybe it's a combination of all three."

She puffed on her pipe and the room filled with smoke.

"So," she added, "would you like

to help an old lady with her shopping after school tomorrow?"

His eyes widened.

"But I won't be able to stop him," he muttered.

"Not with that attitude, you won't. But let's do some training first, to see what you're capable of. Are you feeling peckish? Because I have a scrumptious slice of hazelnut tart for you."

CHAPTER TWENTY

Walter ate every last delicious crumb of the hazelnut tart and sat in the armchair, waiting to become Squirrel Boy. When the transformation happened – it still felt weird, but he was kind of getting used to it by now – he followed her into the garden.

She directed him to the far end, where the fence and some leafy trees hid him from the view of any neighbours, including, most importantly, his mum.

Mrs Onions stood about five metres

away, with a bucket of tennis balls at her feet and, in her hand, an old wooden tennis racquet.

"Don't I get a racquet?" asked Squirrel Boy.

"Certainly not," she said. "We're testing your reflexes, not training you for Wimbledon. The Bogeyman," she explained, "uses balls of mucus as weapons."

"Mucus?"

"Snot."

"Oh. Yuck."

"And, as I don't have any snotballs handy, I'm very happy to say, today we're going to be using tennis balls. I'll be firing them at you, and you'll try to protect yourself, either by dodging them, or by using your tail as a shield."

"Okay," he said, smiling. Being half-squirrel always made him feel more confident, but even plain old Walter wouldn't have worried about being hurt by a tennis ball hit at him by a seventy-three-year-old woman.

She picked up a ball.

"Ready?"

He nodded.

With very little backswing, Mrs Onions smashed the ball at him. When he saw it hurtling towards him, he flinched, but it was too late: the ball thumped into his chest and made him stumble backwards.

"Ow!"

"Sorry," she said, although she had a huge grin on her face as she picked up another ball. "I have played a bit of tennis before," she admitted. "I should have mentioned that. Never underestimate your opponent, Walter. Are you ready this time?"

He nodded again.

The next shot was a ferocious top-spin forehand that whacked him on the shoulder.

"Ouch!" he said.

"Footwork," she told him. "Bounce on your toes. Get your tail ready to block."

When the next ball zoomed towards him, he ducked and it whizzed just past his ear. The next, aimed at his knees, he managed to leap over, surprising himself with just how high he could jump. He was still congratulating himself when the following ball whacked into his tummy. When the next ball hurtled towards him, though, he half-turned and batted it away with his tail.

"Good block," she said. "Now try standing still. No ducking. No weaving. Just use the tail to defend yourself."

She fired balls at him, rat-a-tat.

One hit him in the thigh, and another glanced off the top of his head, but the tail flicked and swished and shielded him from ball after speeding ball.

When the bucket was empty, Mrs Onions bent over and leaned on her racquet, exhausted.

"I enjoyed that," wheezed Mrs Onions. "I haven't played tennis since the French Open, forty-five years ago. I was knocked out in the second round by a Bulgarian. Now, let's see how fast you can collect those balls."

The tennis balls were dotted around the garden, and Squirrel Boy darted about, stooping and plucking them, amazed at just how quick he could go. When he dropped the last ball into the bucket at her feet, she nodded. He was out of breath now, too.

"Okay," she said. "You can defend yourself. And you're really quite nimble. Now it's time to work on your attack. Come inside. Follow me."

CHAPTER TWENTY-ONE

Squirrel Boy followed Mrs Onions into the spare room, which was small and crammed with boxes and strange objects: there was a huge vase in the corner; a human skeleton; and a helmet from a suit of armour. Next to the sewing machine were a wetsuit and an artist's easel. And behind that, the thing that she was looking for: a mannequin.

"Could you carry Antonio outside please, Walter?"

"Antonio?"

"I was a fashion designer for a short while," she explained. "Designers need a dummy to try their clothes on. Antonio was my dummy."

Antonio was six feet tall and very heavy for someone made of plastic, but Squirrel Boy had the strength of a body-builder and, at Mrs Onions' request, carried the mannequin outside with ease and stood him in the garden.

"Now what?" he said.

"Now I want you to attack Antonio," Mrs Onions said, calmly.

Squirrel Boy hesitated. As Walter, he had never hit anybody, not even someone plastic.

"It's okay," she reassured him, smiling.

"Mannequins can't feel pain."

He stepped three paces back from Antonio, took a deep breath, and then launched himself at the dummy.

There was a tangle of arms and legs – real ones and plastic – as they landed in a clumsy heap on the grass. Somehow, Antonio had ended up on top, and Squirrel Boy had a plastic elbow digging into his chest.

Mrs Onions was hooting with laughter.

"It looks like Antonio won the first round," she said, wiping her eyes. "Well, I see you're not much of a fighter, young man."

He struggled to his feet, blushed, and straightened Antonio up.

"If fighting isn't your forte," said Mrs

Onions, "what about dancing?"

He shook his head. At school discos he always steered clear of the dance floor.

"No matter," she continued, breezily. "I taught ballet, many years ago, so I can teach you how to pirouette." She saw the blank look on his face. "It means spinning around quickly. First, you put your feet like this. Then, spring from your toes. Your arms should go like this, and your head needs to move like this to stop you getting dizzy."

He tried it, landed flat on his face, and sighed: he was beginning to get used to the taste of grass. It took him ten tries before he could do it and even then it was a very clumsy pirouette indeed.

"Not bad," said Mrs Onions. "Now do

it again, and this time try to flick your tail around in mid-air and whack Antonio with it."

He took his position, concentrated and then leapt. He spun and thrust his tail out. It brushed the head of the dummy, who wobbled, but stayed upright.

Mrs Onions didn't look very impressed.

"I want you to attack him, Walter," she said, "not tickle him. This time, I want you to imagine that he's a baddy. Is there someone at school who isn't kind to you?"

"There's a boy called Adam Botham," he told her. "He picks on little kids, and he calls me 'Teapot.'"

"Teapot?"

"From my last name: Kettle."

She couldn't stop herself from smiling.

"So," she said in a serious voice, "I want you to imagine that this here is no longer Antonio. He is Adam Botham. He's been bullying small kids, calling you 'Teapot' and also saying awful things about your mother."

Without a moment's hesitation this time, Squirrel Boy sprang at the dummy, eyes wide, his body spinning and his tail whipping around in a blur of movement. It knocked the dummy's head clean off.

He landed on all fours and then stood up.

Mrs Onions looked at Antonio's head on the grass, and then at Squirrel Boy, with a huge smile on her face.

"I do believe you're ready, young man," she said.

CHAPTER TWENTY-TWO

Walter and Mrs Onions walked to the EasyBuy the following afternoon after school... very slowly, because of Mrs Onions' knees. When they got there, she needed a rest, and sagged onto a bench just outside the supermarket, which had an excellent view of the twelve busy checkouts.

Walter sat next to her, feeling incredibly tense. He'd been feeling like that all day at school, unable to concentrate on anything, and the longer he waited outside the bustling supermarket, the more anxious he got. Mrs Onions was making small talk to calm him, but he wasn't really listening. He started hoping that they'd got it wrong about The Bogeyman's alphabet plan, or that he had found another store to rob that began with E.

At that moment, however, in the canned vegetable aisle, pretending to scrutinise tins of mushy peas, was the lanky figure of Jeremy Winkleman-Grubb. His left hand was gripping an empty shopping bag. As for his right hand, well... he extended his index finger, stared at it as if it was a deadly weapon, and then inserted it into his right nostril. Then he went back to pretending to browse the canned peas, waiting for the change.

When grown-ups go to the supermarket, they are usually so preoccupied with checking their lists and choosing what to put in their trolleys that they become practically blind to other people, and so it was several minutes before anyone noticed, and even then it was a toddler in a trolley who spotted him. She yelped in fear and tugged her dad's sleeve, and then he yelped too. That got the attention of a woman nearby, who let out a piercing scream, and after that it didn't take long for the pandemonium to spread like a wave, from aisle to aisle.

On hearing the first squeals, Walter popped a handful of peanuts into his mouth, quickly chobbled them, swallowed and, still sitting, mentally prepared for action.

He took a deep breath as he watched people suddenly going crazy in the supermarket: trolleys crashing and shoppers fleeing.

Mrs Onions gently patted his knee and was whispering something reassuring, but when The Bogeyman came into view she stopped mid-sentence.

Walter gasped.

The Bogeyman was a horrible yellowy green colour, was oozing slime, and strode towards the checkouts.

Men, women and children ran away, skidding and slipping in his icky trail.

"Idiots!" cursed the Bogeyman in a loud, nasal voice. "Brainless imbeciles! Headless chickens!"

A huge arm snaked out towards the first

till, opened it and grabbed a big handful of money while the checkout lady – whose name badge said 'Doreen' – stood wide-eyed and motionless from fright.

After he'd stuffed the money in his bag, he did the same at the second till, and the third. All the while, shoppers and staff were running for cover, and Walter was sitting impatiently on the bench, waiting for the transformation to happen. What if peanuts didn't work? he thought, suddenly. He hadn't tried them before.

After the fourth cash register had been emptied, an old security guard with a grey moustache bravely bustled over to tackle the thief, but the Bogeyman saw him coming. He shot out an extending leg, tripping him up. The guard clattered into a display of sardine tins and stayed there, stuck to the floor with goo, writhing like a caught fish.

The Bogeyman chuckled to himself and stretched out an arm to raid the fifth till as if nothing had happened.

It was then that Walter felt the tickle and the burn.

"It's happening," he muttered.

"Good luck, young man," said Mrs Onions, and he stood up and pulled on the mask, after checking that no one was looking at him. He needn't have worried, though: everyone was either staring at The Bogeyman or running away. Not one person noticed Squirrel Boy walking through the automatic doors and into the supermarket.

CHAPTER TWENTY-THREE

When Walter became Squirrel Boy, it was not only his tail and claws that grew; it was his confidence, too. But there was still a nervous wobble in his voice as he bounded over to the checkouts and called out:

"Stop! Put that money back!"

The Bogeyman paused his stretchy arm in mid-air, looked down at Squirrel Boy and snorted with laughter.

"Who are you?" he sneered. "Guinea

Pig Kid?"

"Squirrel Boy."

"Squirrel Boy?" The Bogeyman said, roaring with laughter as if he'd just repeated the punchline to a particularly hilarious joke. "Ha ha! You've even got a funny little tail! Oh, delicious, delicious!"

"I said: Put.The. Money. Back!"

There was a moment's silence, and then The Bogeyman burst into laughter again.

"Haven't you got a tree to go to?" he said to Squirrel Boy. "And, talking of trees... I need to leave."

The Bogeyman chuckled at his joke, scraped goo off his body and flicked a huge bogey at Squirrel Boy – much bigger than a tennis ball, Squirrel Boy realised as it flew towards him – more melon-sized.

He dived behind the checkout at the last moment. The ball whizzed past him and hit the supermarket window, spraying yellow-green goo everywhere.

When Squirrel Boy sprang up again, the Bogeyman pelted another disgusting ball at him, and this time he spun around and blocked it with his tail, splattering more slime.

"Now you've made me angry," announced Squirrel Boy. "That's snot a good idea."

He bounded over the checkout and launched at the Bogeyman, dodging his flailing arms until he got to him and tried to grab his elastic body, but the Bogeyman was much too flexible. It was like trying to attack a huge, powerful rubber band. Squirrel Boy bounced off him spectacularly, his own speed propelling him rapidly sideways through the air until he crashed into a huge pyramid of cornflakes packets, three aisles away.

He was winded, flat on his back, with cornflakes stuck to him with icky goo. And, before he could even try to struggle back to his feet and wipe himself down, he saw the Bogeyman racing out of the supermarket, grinning triumphantly, with the bag of money in his grasp, snatching a few chocolate bars as he left, and leaving chaos in his wake.

CHAPTER TWENTY-FOUR

As they'd agreed beforehand, Squirrel Boy bounded back to Mrs Onions' house as fast as he could, down the backstreets, making sure that nobody saw him. He sneaked into her back garden and hid in a bush, waiting for her to come home.

She took so long that he'd transformed back into Walter – a gooey, cornflakey, shivering Walter – when she unlocked the back door and peered out looking for him.

"Come in, wherever you are," she said

softly and, when she saw the state that he was in, added: "Perhaps you should leave your shoes on the step, young man, so I can clean them."

He sighed and took off his sticky shoes before trudging into the house, feeling a mix of emotions but none of them good: embarrassed, sore, exhausted.

"You hop in the shower," said Mrs Onions in a cheery voice, "and I'll put your clothes in the drier. You can wear my dressing gown while you're waiting, and I'll make you one of my special hot chocolates. I'll call your mum now to ask her if you can stay a bit later. I'll tell her we're watching a film."

He nodded, too tired to protest, or even to talk.

Half an hour later, as if he hadn't suffered enough humiliation for one day, he found himself sitting in an armchair in Mrs Onions' front room, wearing nothing but a pink, old-fashioned dressing gown.

She came in from the kitchen, handed him a steaming mug of hot chocolate and sat opposite him.

"I'm very proud of you, young man. You tried your very best. And you were successful, too. In a way."

Walter frowned. He knew she was trying to be positive, but no amount of positivity could call what happened in the supermarket a success.

"Really," she continued, "if you hadn't intervened, he would have raided all of those tills. He left much earlier that he'd planned, I'm sure, and it was all thanks to you."

Walter nodded, but it didn't make him feel any better. The hot chocolate was helping his mood a tiny bit, however; he sipped it and it slipped down his throat, warming him from the inside.

They were quiet for a few minutes before Walter spoke.

"Where do you think he'll go next?"

"A place that has even more money than a supermarket," she said.

"A bank?"

She nodded.

"Specifically," she said, "the Federal Bank, in town. But, knowing where he'll go, and stopping him, are two very different things. In fact, there might be nothing that anyone can do to stop him," she added, sadly. "Not even the police. Perhaps, like an actual bogey, he's indestructible, too."

When his clothes were dry, Walter got dressed and went home. His mum was watching the news on TV.

"The Bogeyman struck at the EasyBuy," she announced, breathlessly. "And you won't believe this, but there was some kind of a Squirrel superhero who tried to stop him."

Walter pretended to be shocked.

"Well," she said, correcting herself, "maybe not a superhero. More like a quite-good-hero. He didn't actually stop the Bogeyman. They had a fight, and the squirrel came second."

Walter sighed.

"It's late," she said. "You look exhausted. Time for bed." She kissed him. "Sweet dreams," she said, but his dreams were full of humiliation and disgusting goo, and were anything but sweet.

CHAPTER TWENTY-FIVE

The next day was Friday and Walter had a long day at school. He even fell asleep in Science. The teacher rapped a wooden ruler on his desk, Walter woke up with a start, and everyone giggled. Walter blushed. If only they knew what he'd been doing the night before, he thought. Actually, it was very good they didn't know, he realised. In the playground, everyone was talking excitedly about the events of last night. A group of older boys were debating if Squirrel Boy was the lamest superhero ever. In art class, a girl drew a picture: Squirrel Boy was depicted sprawled on the floor, with the Bogeyman's foot on his chest.

After school, feeling incredibly fed up, Walter went to visit Mrs Onions. She sat in her favourite armchair, drinking tea and puffing away at her pipe, with the TV on but the sound turned down.

She'd bought all the newspapers and spread them out on the dining room table. Walter miserably scanned all the front pages.

There was a grainy picture of him – well, Squirrel Boy – in every paper. Someone at the supermarket must have taken it with their phone, but the mask had worked; you couldn't tell that Squirrel Boy was actually Walter Kettle. He sighed with relief.

The *Daily Mirror*'s front page was:

The *Daily Star*'s headline was:

Even the *Financial Times*, which usually just had stories about business and stock markets and other incredibly boring stuff, had the story on its front page:

FINANCIAL TIMES

Half-Man-Half-Mucus defeats Half-Boy-Half-Squirrel in Supermarket Incident

"You're famous," Mrs Onions said.

"Famous for being a loser," he muttered.

Then there was a newsflash on TV. Mrs Onions quickly turned up the volume and

THE BOGEYMAN STRIKES AGAIN··· THIS TIME AT THE FEDERAL BANK ON THE HIGH STREET···

THE POLICE ARRIVED AT THE SCENE···

AND FIRED AT HIM···

BUT HE EASILY DODGED THE BULLETS···

AND ESCAPED WITH HIS LARGEST HAUL YET.

they both stared at it, open-mouthed.

"See!" said Mrs Onions. "I told you. Even the police couldn't stop him. What chance have we?"

"With that attitude," said Walter, "we have no chance at all."

She grinned at him. He smiled: a faint smile, but the best he'd been able to manage all day.

"I deserved that," she said.

And then she sneezed.

She wiped her nose with a hanky that had been balled up in her cardigan sleeve.

This gave Walter his brilliant idea.

"Maybe we can beat him," he said. "Mrs Onions, could you do some sewing, please?"

She looked puzzled.

"What do you have in mind?" she asked, and then grinned delightedly when he told her his plan. "It's certainly worth a try," she said.

"Do you know where he'll be tomorrow?" asked Walter.

"I think so," she said, and slowly got up from her armchair, fetched a newspaper from the table and handed it to him. "Page fourteen," she said. "At the bottom."

The headline was so small that it took him a while to find it:

Rare Congolese Diamond On Show In Museum

"But 'museum' begins with an 'M'," he pointed out. "He's only up to G, remember."

"It has a lot of paintings," she said, her eyes twinkling with excitement. "Its full name is 'Gallery and Museum'. Do you fancy going there with me tomorrow? I hear it's quite educational."

CHAPTER TWENTY-SIX

The next morning was Saturday and Walter woke up really early, but when he went to get breakfast, his mum was already there, tapping away on her computer, with a big smile on her face.

"What's up?" said Walter, sleepily. "Why so happy?"

"Well," she said, "not only have I got the best son ever, who is keeping a lonely old lady company, but today my blog has had the most hits ever. It's 'trending', whatever that means."

Writing the blog was one of his mum's roles for Friends of the Animals. The more people that looked at it, the better it was for the charity, so she was always trying to come up with interesting animal stories to write about.

"It's called 'Who is Squirrel Boy?'" she announced. "And it seems to be the question on everybody's lips."

It's not on my lips, thought Walter as he poured himself a bowl of bran flakes.

"I've had 159 comments already," his mum continued.

"What are they saying?" he asked, trying not to look too interested.

"Well," she said, not taking her eyes off the computer screen, "some people think he's just a strange kid who likes dressing up. There's another theory that he's actually an alien. And one person called 'Conspiracy123' thinks that the government tried to create a person-squirrel hybrid and it somehow escaped from the lab."

"And what do you think, Mum?"

She looked up from the screen and shrugged.

"I'm not sure," she said. "I am intrigued, though, and I'm going to investigate. If I can be the one to find out who – or what – he is, just imagine the publicity that Friends of the Animals would get!"

He sighed inwardly, but knew that when his mum made up her mind to do something, she couldn't be talked out of it. He'd just have to be even more careful to keep it a secret.

"What would you like to do today, Walter?"

He shrugged.

"I was going to visit Mrs Onions."

"Again?"

"Is that okay, Mum?"

"Of course it is," she said. "It's great that you're looking after her."

Walter nodded, thinking that it was the other way around: Mrs Onions was looking after him; it was the whole town that he was trying to look after.

CHAPTER TWENTY-SEVEN

They arrived at the museum just after opening time – Mrs Onions with her handbag, Walter carrying a heavy shopping bag – and they went straight to the Congolese diamond. It was really impressive: the size of a plum, sparkly and enclosed in a glass case. The glass was thick, but Walter doubted that it would be enough to stop the Bogeyman.

Mrs Onions had insisted that they had a quick look around while they were waiting. Walter had never been to the museum before, and he might have found it fascinating if he hadn't been so nervous. Mrs Onions explained what everything was; she knew a lot about really old things, which Walter guessed was probably because she was extremely old herself.

After they'd seen most of the exhibits, they went to the museum café, where they sat at a small table which had a good view of the diamond.

Mrs Onions bought a cup of tea for herself, and a vanilla milkshake for Walter.

Then they waited.

And waited some more.

Then they waited even more than that.

And then it was lunchtime, so Mrs

Onions ordered burgers for both of them. Actual burgers, not chick pea ones. Walter enjoyed his burger so much that, for a few minutes, he even forgot to be nervous.

But a few minutes later, Walter felt jumpy again. Even though he'd just eaten, his tummy felt as light as a balloon.

He started to wonder if the Bogeyman would turn up, and rather hoped that he wouldn't. 'Gold' began with G. Was there a gold shop somewhere? Or a golf course? There would be a lot of rich golfers to steal from.

It was then that Walter noticed a strange man lurking by the diamond exhibit. The man was lanky and fidgety and wearing a hat with the brim pulled down low, so you couldn't see his eyes. But you could see him picking his nose. Walter nudged Mrs Onions to get her attention.

"He looks suspicious, don't you think?" Walter said.

"It could be him," she said, squinting. And then: "It must be. Look! He's turning a funny colour."

Taking a deep breath, Walter took the packet of salted peanuts from his pocket, emptied the contents into his mouth, chewed, swallowed, and waited for the change to happen.

Meanwhile, Jeremy Winkleman-Grubb was transforming into the Bogeyman right in front of their eyes. His face and hands were already green and slimy, and his body was stretching. He stepped over to the case, slid a stretchy arm through the tiniest join in the glass, and plucked the diamond from its stand.

But how would the Bogeyman get it out of the case, Walter wondered? He soon had the answer.

Diamonds are many times stronger than glass, and the Bogeyman was using the diamond itself to cut a hole in the case.

An alarm was going off by this time – whoop! whoop! whoop! – and there was pandemonium in the museum. People were running in all directions, terrified.

Two security guards rushed over to grab the Bogeyman. There was a brief scuffle, but he squirmed out of their grasp and shoved them backwards. Suddenly the guards were sprawled on the wooden floor, dazed, and covered in sticky goo, unable to move.

The Bogeyman went back to stealing the diamond as if nothing had happened and, after only a minute, he'd finished cutting a circle of glass, popped the diamond out of the hole, and grabbed it with his other hand.

As all this was happening, Walter was waiting impatiently for his own transformation.

At last, he felt the familiar twitching and tingling, put on his mask and jumped up, carrying the shopping bag. Then he sprinted over to the Bogeyman and shouted:

"Put the diamond down, and your hands up!"

The Bogeyman looked mildly irritated.

"If it isn't Gerbil Boy again," he sighed, "back for more punishment. You should have stayed home in your cage."

"It's you who should be behind bars," said Squirrel Boy.

"Bullets bounce off me," he bragged. "What chance has a pathetic little squirrel?"

He let out a horrible, gurgly laugh and flung a huge ball of snot in Walter's direction. When he saw it speeding towards him, Walter dived behind a sculpture.

Splat!

The sculpture was now covered in slime.

Crouching, Walter opened the shopping bag, and yanked out its contents: two white double-bed sheets that Mrs Onions had sewn together the night before.

In one movement, he spread open the huge sheet, sprang out from behind the sculpture and bounded over towards the

Bogeyman, who tried to duck but wasn't quick enough. Squirrel Boy pounced on him with the giant bedsheet and smothered him.

They toppled over in the wild struggle. Squirrel Boy winced as punches and kicks caught him. The Bogeyman writhed and wriggled, his arms and legs flailing, but eventually he was wrapped up completely in the bedsheet and his resistance slowly ebbed away.

"I was wondering what could possibly stop a giant bogey," Squirrel Boy said to him, triumphantly. "An enormous hankie, that's what!"

The Bogeyman was still trying to squirm out, but Squirrel Boy knew that the gigantic handkerchief had sapped most of his enemy's strength, and that all he had to do now was stay on top of it until the police arrived.

But someone had other ideas: Violet Winkleman-Grubb; the Bogeyman's mum.

CHAPTER TWENTY-EIGHT

Violet Winkleman-Grubb had been standing in the corner of the room, watching proudly as her snot-covered supervillain son removed the diamond.

But when Squirrel Boy attacked him with the huge handkerchief, her smile vanished.

She armed herself with a Ming period vase and crept up behind Squirrel Boy, scowling.

He didn't notice her at all: he was

too busy trying to stop her son from wriggling free.

When she was right behind him, she lifted the vase above her head, and…

Mrs Onions had got up from her seat and was watching on – at first, anxiously, and then with pride – but she gasped when she spotted the fat lady waddling over, sneaking up behind Squirrel Boy, brandishing the vase.

What followed was a very low-speed chase, like a real-life slow-motion replay.

As Violet Winkleman-Grubb waddled towards Squirrel Boy, Mrs Onions shuffled over to her and…

Just as the vase was about to crack into the back of Squirrel Boy's head, Mrs Onions unleashed an almighty karate chop into the fat lady's side. It was only one blow, but it was enough to make Violet Winkleman-Grubb double over and collapse into a heap onto the museum floor. She let go of the vase and Mrs Onions caught it before it could hit the floor.

They could hear sirens from police cars getting louder and louder and, as soon as the police arrived, Squirrel Boy hopped off the handkerchief.

Three policemen and two policewomen unwrapped the hankie and hand-cuffed the contents... by now, no longer the Bogeyman, but just Jeremy Winkleman-Grubb.

As the police bustled him – and his mother – away to the police station,

the people in the museum applauded
and cheered.

But Squirrel Boy and Mrs Onions had
already gone.

CHAPTER TWENTY-NINE

The Winkleman-Grubbs were sent to prison for a really long time.

The forensic scientists were able to work out how Jeremy Winkleman-Grubb had made the transformations, so they made sure he was handcuffed all day and all night, his hands behind his back, to make nose-picking impossible.

But what about Walter Kettle?

Well, he went back to his normal life, pretty much, except that every Saturday morning, he went next door to visit Mrs Onions. She'd sit in her favourite armchair, smoking a pipe and drinking tea, and would always bring him delicious food to eat, and homemade lemonade or milkshake to drink.

They would chat: about Walter's school or, more often, about Mrs Onions' amazing life, as chronicled by all the photos on the wall in her front room.

She'd recently added two more framed pictures, and this time they weren't of her. They were newspaper front pages from the day after the museum incident.

WE'RE NUTS ABOUT SQUIRREL BOY
Young Superhero Saves Diamond

And:

BYE BYE, BOGEY

Also:

RODENT SUPERHERO SPARKLES, WIPES OUT BOGEYMAN
(WITH MYSTERY PENSIONER'S HELP)

The photos that accompanied the headlines were clearer this time, but thankfully not clear enough for Walter to be identified, even by his own mother. The old lady in the photos did look kind of like Mrs Onions, it was true, but lots of old ladies looked that way, and so no one suspected her.

On this particular Saturday, Mrs Onions had brought Walter a yummy looking rectangular slice of homemade cake on a plate, with some of her excellent lemonade to wash it down.

"Thanks," he said, licking his lips.

"It's almond slice," she said.

He frowned.

"But almonds... they're nuts, aren't they?"

"Yes," she admitted. "I've got a little job for you, Walter."

He sighed.

"Is there a new supervillain in town?" he asked.

"Not exactly," she said. "To be honest, I've just got some high shelves that need dusting. I could use your climbing ability, and that amazing tail of yours."

Walter sighed, then smiled and took a bite out of the cake. It was delicious.

He didn't mind being a squirrel, occasionally. He'd beaten the Bogeyman and saved the town, so a little bit of housework would be no match for…
SQUIRREL BOY!

THE END

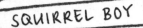

SQUIRREL BOY

1

AGE: 10
BUSHINESS OF TAIL: 96
NIBBLING ABILITY: 93
SIZE OF BOGEYS: 3
SPEED: 78
SPECIAL POWERS:
speed, agility, sense of smell.

AKA Walter Kettle

ANGELA KETTLE

4

AGE: 31
BUSHINESS OF TAIL: 0
NIBBLING ABILITY: 18
SIZE OF BOGEYS: 1
SPEED: 27
SPECIAL POWERS:
spotting dirt from a long distance, detecting failure to brush teeth.

AKA Walter's mum

THE BOGEYMAN

3

AGE: 33
BUSHINESS OF TAIL: 0
NIBBLING ABILITY: 9
SIZE OF BOGEYS: 99
SPEED: 74
SPECIAL POWERS:
Snotballs, flexibility.

AKA Jeremy Winkleman-Grubb

MRS ONIONS

2

AGE: Mind Your Own Business
BUSHINESS OF TAIL: Excuse me?!
NIBBLING ABILITY: 23
SIZE OF BOGEYS: I beg your pardon
SPEED: 4
SPECIAL POWERS:
baking, sewing, karate.

AKA The Old Lady Next Door

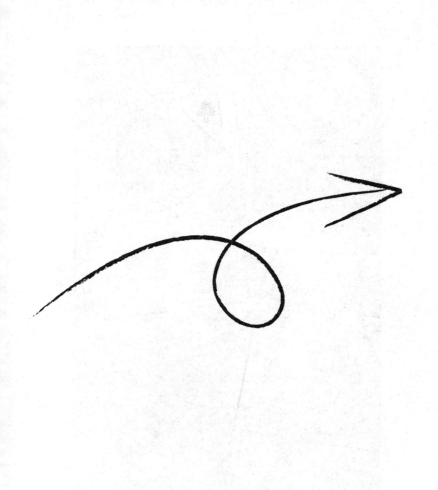

Coming soon from a superhero near you…

CHAPTER ONE

Have you ever noticed how some dog owners are exactly like their dogs?

The Box family, for example, have a labrador called Porky who is so lazy that he can't be bothered chasing cats: he just glares at them and hopes they get the message. The Box family are just as lazy: they spend an awful lot of time glued to the TV. Even getting up from the sofa to go to the toilet seems like a huge hassle.

Jack Gunderson's Jack Russell, Russell,

on the other hand, is too lively. He can't stop yapping, and neither, for that matter, can Jack Gunderson himself: he talks to everyone he meets and goes on endlessly about the same three boring subjects:

1. the weather
2. how much better things used to be in the old days, and
3. how much better the weather used to be in the old days.

But this story isn't about Jack Gunderson, or the Boxes.

Which is very lucky, because a story about the Boxes would be very boring indeed. Nothing would happen at all apart from them eating, burping, scratching and watching the telly. And a story about Jack Gunderson would just be him banging on and on about how rainy it's been; or how, when he was a kid, you could go to the movies for a few pennies, have a box of popcorn the size of a small building, and still have enough change left over to buy a medium-sized country.

No, this story is – at least partly – about a man called Auberon Steyn, and his dog, Snarl.

As you might guess by the name, Snarl isn't one of those cute little fluffy puppies that sits in your lap and licks your face.

Snarl is much too big for anyone's lap. And he isn't a licker.

Oh, no.

He's a biter.

And as for his owner, Auberon Steyn,

he is small and podgy, he waddles when he walks, and he's quite possibly the most horrible man in the entire town.

CHAPTER TWO

There is no nice way to say this: Auberon Steyn liked killing things.

In Africa, there are men called 'Big-Game Hunters'. These are men with very big guns and very small brains, who think it's fun to shoot incredible beasts such as lions and elephants and cheetahs – animals who have done absolutely nothing to them – and mount the dead animals' heads on plaques, or make rugs out of their fur, and use them to decorate their big, stupid houses.

In the town where Auberon Steyn lived there were no lions or elephants or anything like that. But that didn't stop him from hunting things.

Auberon Steyn was a Small-Game Hunter.

He caught badgers and bunnies and birds. Any wild animal that moved – and some, like hedgehogs, that hardly moved at all – were fair game for Auberon Steyn.

But the animal he took the most pleasure in killing was the squirrel.

His house was full of trophies, but not trophies as you and I would know them. His trophies were not made of metal; they were badger heads on plaques, hedgehog -quill toothpicks and, most of all, squirrel tails. Hundreds of them, lining his walls.

To be continued...